caw

coo chuck

tat tzik

dee

chuck

chip

tat

tat tat

h qua qua qua

qua

de aw

h dee W

tzik

dee

coo tzik

birdsongs

tzik

chip
chip

chip
chip

betsy franco
steve jenkins

bird
songs

MARGARET K. McELDERRY BOOKS
NEW YORK LONDON TORONTO SYDNEY

E
FRA

Margaret K. McElderry Books · An imprint of Simon & Schuster Children's Publishing Division · 1230 Avenue of the Americas, New York, New York 10020 · Text copyright © 2007 by Betsy Franco · Illustrations copyright © 2007 by Steve Jenkins · All rights reserved, including the right of reproduction in whole or in part in any form. Book design by Sonia Chaghatzbanian · The text for this book is set in Filosofia. · The illustrations for this book are collage. · Manufactured in China · 10 9 8 7 6 5 4 3 2 1 Library of Congress Cataloging-in-Publication Data · Franco, Betsy. · Birdsongs / Betsy Franco ; illustrated by Steve Jenkins.—1st ed. · p. cm. Summary: Throughout the day and into the night, various birds sing their songs, beginning with the woodpecker who taps a pole ten times and counting down to the hummingbird who calls once. · ISBN-13: 978-0-689-87777-3 · ISBN-10: 0-689-87777-3 (hardcover) · [1. Birdsongs—Fiction. 2. Birds—Fiction. 3. Day—Fiction. 4. Counting.] I. Jenkins, Steve, 1952– ill. II. Title. · PZ7.F8475Bi 2007 · [E]—dc22 · 2004025056

FIRST
EDITION

For Doug,
who feeds the birds
at our house
—B. F.

For Jeffrey
—S. J.

The sky is quiet. The yard is quiet.

The creek is quietly gurgling.

The rising sun turns the sky

from black to gray to pink to blue.

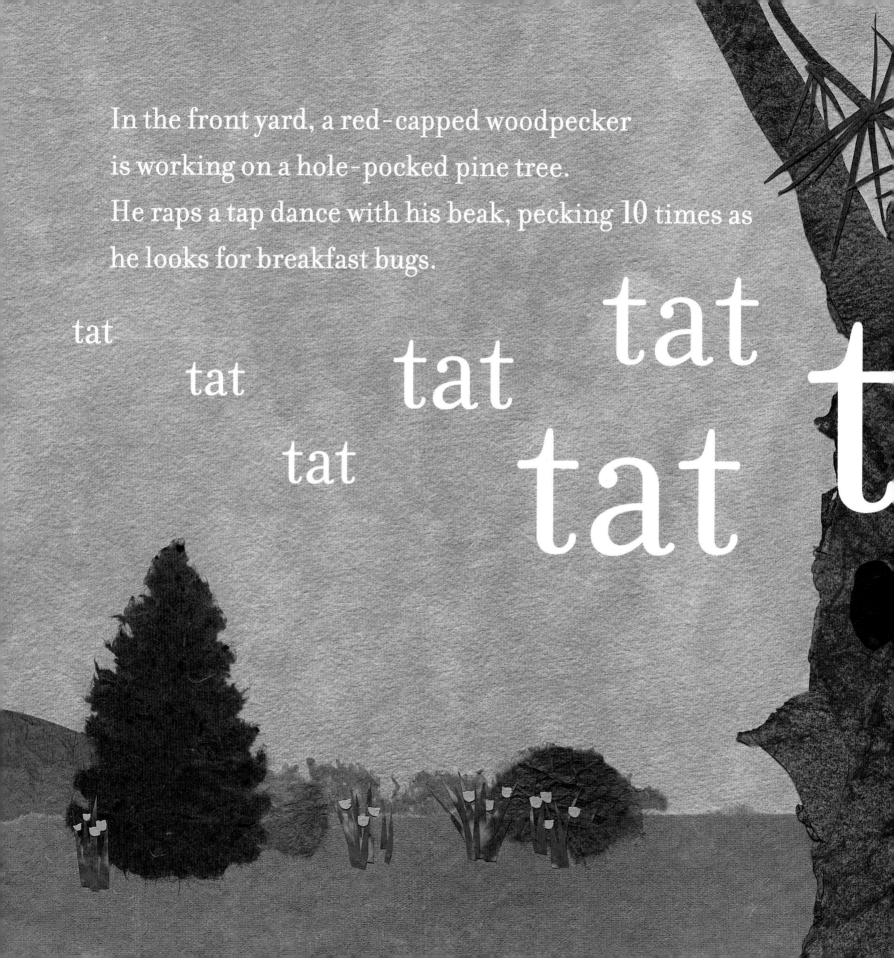

In the front yard, a red-capped woodpecker
is working on a hole-pocked pine tree.
He raps a tap dance with his beak, pecking 10 times as
he looks for breakfast bugs.

tat

tat

tat

tat

tat

tat

tat

t

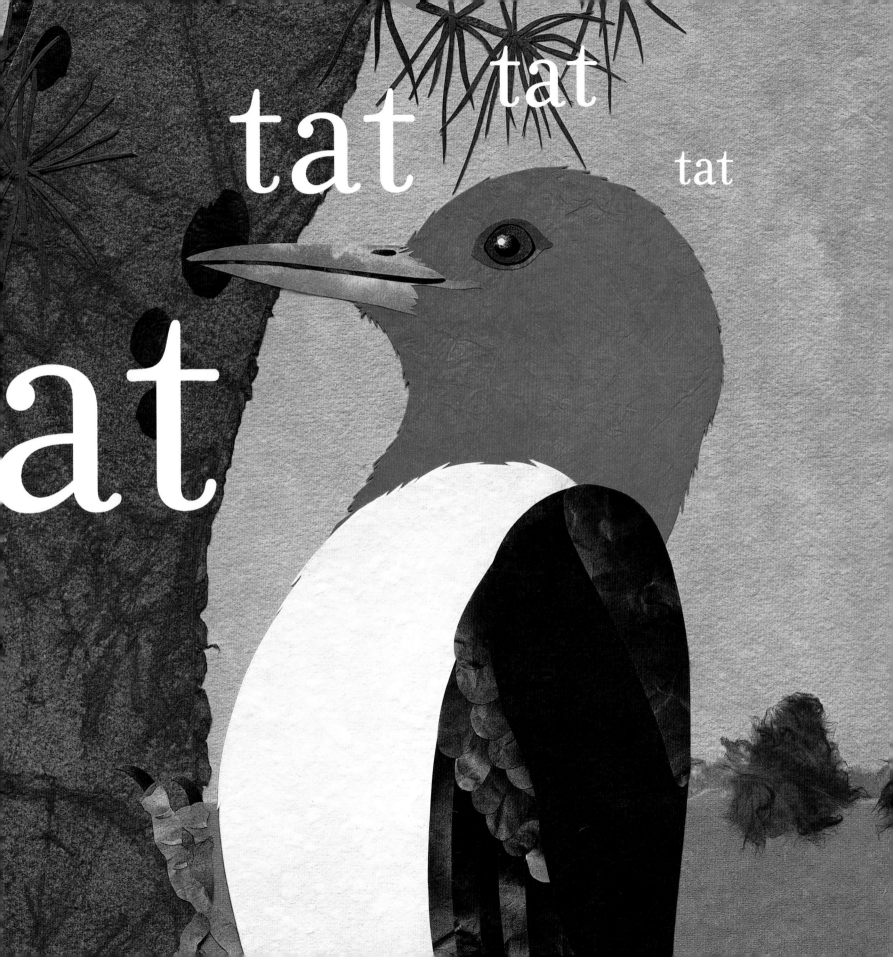

tat

tat

tat

at

A mourning dove lands
on the telephone wire
and folds its gray wings.

More doves find places in line.
Then they dive down to share the
sunflower seeds under the bird feeder,
cooing to one another 9 times.

coo

COO

COO

chip

chip

chip

chip

chip
chip

chip

chip

A flutter. A flurry. A flapping of chipping sparrows.
The sparrows crowd around the bird feeder and poke
one another out of the way, filling the air with 8 sharp notes.
Each one wants to be first in line.

eeyah

eeyah

e

The sun is high in the sky now.

The bottoms of the clouds are fringed with gray.

A white gull from the bay circles over the front yard

and the creek. Its mouth open wide,

the gull warns and nags 7 times that rain is coming.

eeyah

eeyah

eyah

eeyah

eeyah

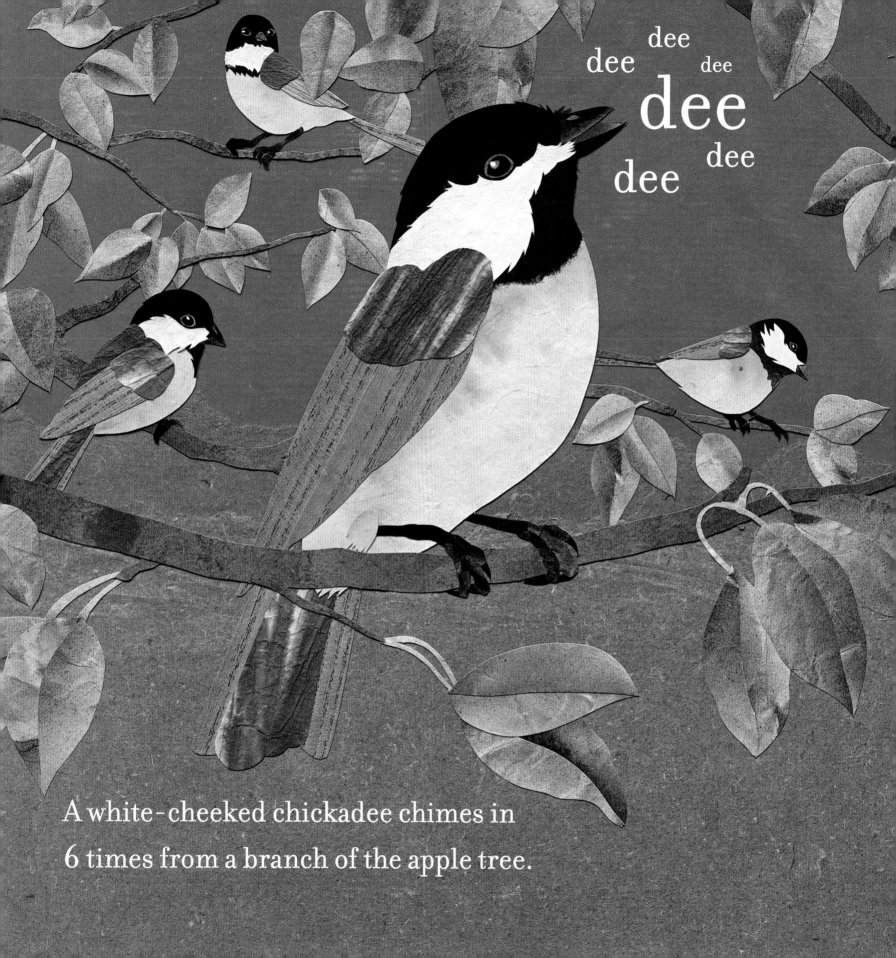

dee dee dee dee dee dee dee

A white-cheeked chickadee chimes in
6 times from a branch of the apple tree.

More and more chickadees join her
until the tree looks like a candelabra.
They fly off in midsong when
the tabby cat starts climbing.

A short rain shower. Dressed in shiny green suits,
mallards in the creek discuss the weather.
"The gull was right," they say,
quacking 5 times in agreement.

qua

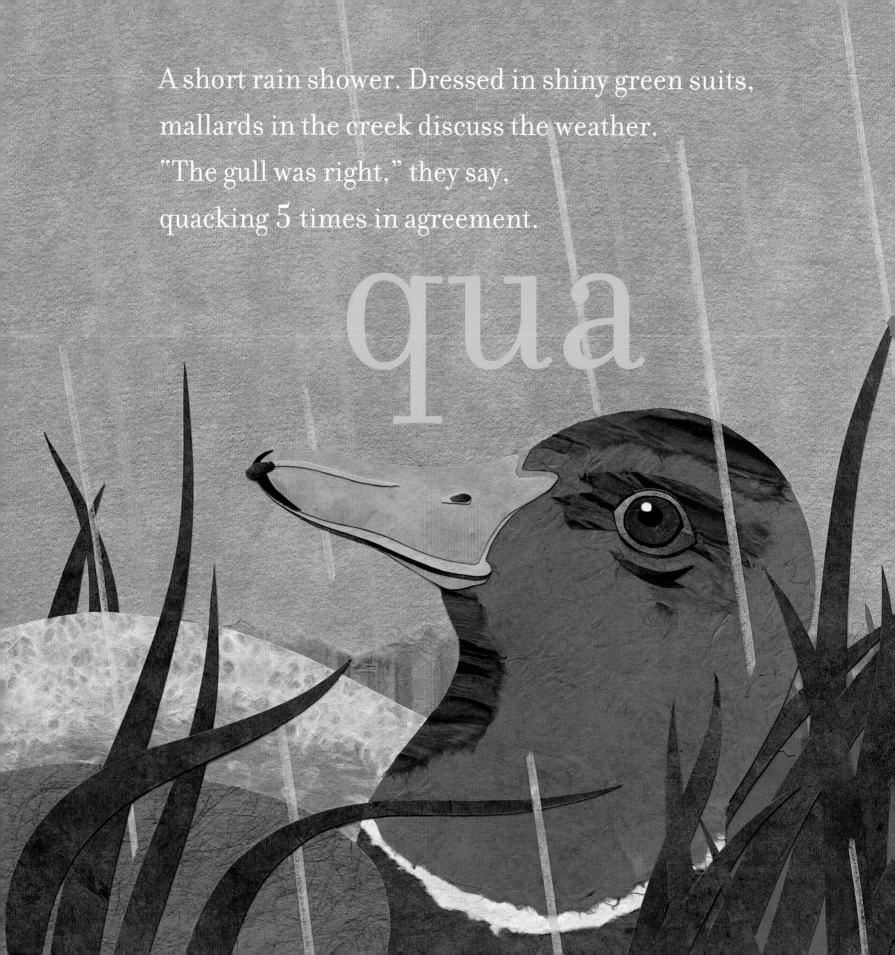

A crow listens in, tottering along the creek fence.
When he takes off, he looks too large to fly.
But his broad black wings carry him up
as he squawks 4 times.

caw

caw

caw

caw

The sun is low now.

Back on the maple tree next to the house,

the robin, heavy with eggs,

settles herself into her nest of bark and grass.

She softly sings 3 notes.

tut

tut

tut

chuck

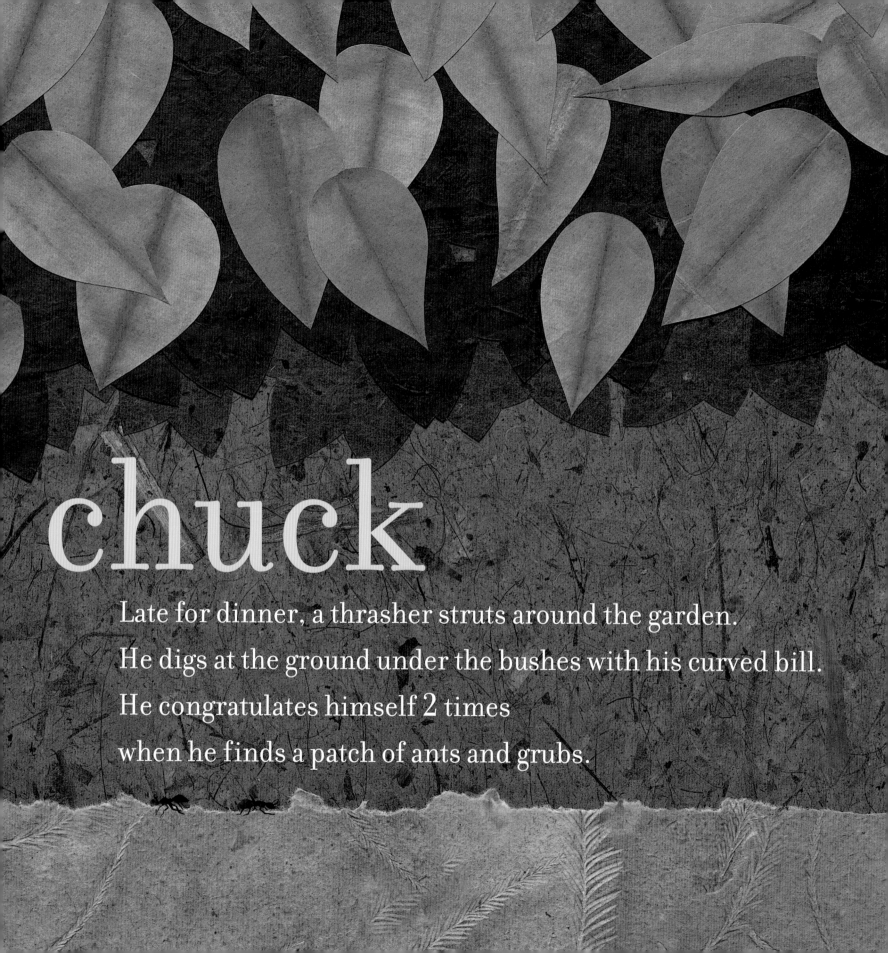

chuck

Late for dinner, a thrasher struts around the garden.

He digs at the ground under the bushes with his curved bill.

He congratulates himself 2 times

when he finds a patch of ants and grubs.

tzik

A hummingbird sucks one last treat
from the trumpet-shaped honeysuckle
in the garden. Her wings look like
a helicopter propeller.
She makes 1 tiny sound
in her high voice.

As the sun sets, it's quiet in the sky.

It's quiet in the yard.

It's quiet in the gurgling creek,

where the moon is reflected in the ripples . . .

. . . until the mockingbird begins to sing from the pine tree. She copies all of the songs and calls she has heard during the day.

tat
chi
chip
tat
e
chuck
chuck
tut tut

feathery facts

Woodpeckers eat all day. Some find tiny insects or larvae in trees and dead wood. Others peck holes in dead trees and telephone poles to store their nuts.

Mourning doves are easy to find all over the United States. Their name comes from their *mournful*, sad birdsong.

When eating their favorite seeds at the bird feeder, some types of **sparrows** don't like to share! They make other birds wait in nearby trees while they eat most of the seeds and leave a mess on the ground.

Gulls are known as the acrobats of the sky. When they catch a breeze in just the right way, it looks like they're floating completely still in midair.

Chickadees are songbirds that live in flocks of about five to twelve birds. One pair of birds are usually the leaders of the flock. The leaders sometimes chase the others around to show who's in charge.

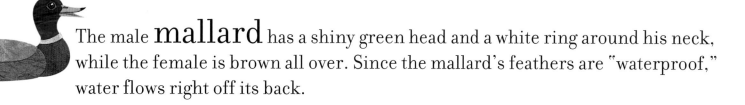

The male **mallard** has a shiny green head and a white ring around his neck, while the female is brown all over. Since the mallard's feathers are "waterproof," water flows right off its back.

Crows perch on tall trees and keep watch to protect one another. When a crow flies, its wingspan can be more than three feet.

A **robin**'s egg is a light blue color. The mother robin fiercely protects her nest while she waits about two weeks for her eggs to hatch.

A **thrasher** busily *thrashes* around in the leaves and twigs with its strong, curved bill, searching for food. It can also dig holes with its bill to find bugs in the soil.

A tiny **hummingbird**'s wings can flap about forty to eighty times in a second. It can hover in the air and even fly backward!

The **mockingbird** can not only imitate the sound of other birds' songs, but it can also copy sounds such as a squeaking door, a barking dog, or even a cell phone.

chip tzik tut

coo eeyah chip

ee eeya

dee
dee tzik
chip coo qua
tat tat tut dee dee dee
coo
coo eeya
tzik tat
tat tut tat
chip chuck coo
chuck tat qua coo coo